The Sleeping Beauty

The Sleeping Beauty

Charles Perrault

Translated and Illustrated by

David Walker

Thomas Y. Crowell Company

New York

For my father and mother

Perrault, Charles, 1628–1703.
  The sleeping beauty.

  Translation of La belle au bois dormant.
  SUMMARY: Disgruntled at not being invited to the
princess' christening, the wicked fairy casts a spell
that dooms the princess to sleep for a hundred years.

(1.   Fairy tales.   2.   Folklore-France)   I.   Walker,

David,   1934–   II.   Title.

PZ8.P426S1   12   (Fic)   76-22697

ISBN 0-690-01278-0
ISBN 0-690-01279-9 (lib. bdg.)

Once upon a time, far away and long ago, there lived a king and queen. They loved each other very much, and had all the riches they could wish for, but still they were unhappy, because they had no children.

Years passed, and at last the queen had a baby daughter. The whole country rejoiced, and the king ordered a great banquet to be held at the castle to celebrate the christening. He invited seven fairies who lived in the land to be godmothers to the little princess. Each fairy was to bring her a precious gift, for that was the custom of the time.

On the day of the christening, the seven fairies sat down among the other guests at the banquet table. Before each fairy was placed a special gift from the king and queen—a golden box in which were a knife, a fork, and a spoon, all set with diamonds and rubies. The musicians started to play, servants scurried to and fro bringing dishes heaped with fine foods to the table, and the banquet began.

Suddenly the door of the great hall was flung open. There in the doorway stood an old, old woman. Everyone turned to look at her. She was a fairy. The king had not sent her an invitation, for he had supposed she must long since have died. Now he hastily ordered a place to be laid for her, but he had no golden box to give her, for only seven had been made.

As the old fairy hobbled to the table she looked furiously angry. She was sure the king had overlooked her on purpose, and she muttered threats and curses. The seventh and youngest fairy, who overheard her, slipped away from the banquet and hid behind a curtain. She thought she might be needed to help the princess if the old fairy tried to do her any harm.

When the banquet ended,
it was time for the fairies to
bestow their gifts on the
princess. The first one gave
her the gift of intelligence;
the second, beauty; the third,
kindness; the fourth,
generosity; the fifth, gaiety;
the sixth, grace.

Then the aged fairy rose, still muttering angrily. The whole court drew back in horror.

"This is my gift to the child," cried the old fairy. "When the princess reaches her sixteenth birthday, she shall prick her finger with the spindle of a spinning wheel, and she shall die!"

But at that very moment the youngest fairy
stepped out from behind the curtain.

"Take comfort, your Majesties," said the
fairy in her clear voice. "The princess will
indeed prick her finger with a spindle,
but she shall not die. Instead, she will
sleep for a hundred years, until she is
awakened by a kiss from a king's son."

The king at once sent out a proclamation
forbidding anyone in the kingdom to use a
spinning wheel or even to keep
a spindle in the house. The
princess grew up as lovely and
sweet-tempered, as generous and
gay and talented as the fairies had
promised, and the king believed her
safe from the old
fairy's wicked spell.

One day, when the princess was nearing her sixteenth birthday, she wandered into a part of the castle where she had never been before. The king and queen were away, and nobody questioned her as she walked down the long, deserted corridors and peered into huge dusty rooms.

At last the princess came to a door at the top of a narrow spiral staircase. She pushed it open and found herself in a little room, where an old woman sat. She had once been a servant at the castle, and because she lived, old and forgotten, in her garret, she had never seen the princess, or heard the king's proclamation.

"What are you doing, old woman?" asked the princess.

"Why, spinning, of course, child!" said the old woman, surprised.

"What is that wheel for?"

"It is a spinning wheel," said the old woman. "Why, you talk as if you had never seen such a thing before."

"I have never even heard of it," said the princess. "Oh, do let me try to spin!"

The kindly old woman handed her the spindle; but as soon as the princess touched it, the spindle pricked her finger and she fell to the floor in a deep sleep.

The old woman cried out in alarm and ran for help. The princess's attendants carried her to the great hall of the castle and sent for the king and queen.

The king was stricken with grief, but he remembered
what the good fairy had said. He gave orders that
the princess should be laid on a bed in the finest
bedchamber in the castle and left in peace until
the time came for her to be awakened.
Deep in her enchanted sleep, the
princess looked more beautiful
than ever.

The king sent at once for the good fairy, who arrived in a chariot drawn by doves. She approved all he had done, but saw that when the princess awoke she would be sad to find herself all alone in the castle. And so she waved her wand, and every living creature in the castle fell asleep: the king and queen, the courtiers and ladies-in-waiting, the cooks and scullions, the pages and footmen—even the princess's little dog Puff, who lay curled up on her bed.

Once more the fairy waved her wand, and trees sprang up all around the castle. Thorny brambles twined themselves so thickly around the walls that no one could get through them, and all but the topmost turrets of the castle were hidden from view.

So the castle slept. Before long the throne passed to another family; and at the end of a hundred years the story of the sleeping princess was all but forgotten.

One day, a king's son happened to be hunting nearby, and caught sight of the towers of the castle. He had never been in that part of the country and had never heard the story. No one could tell him about the castle but an old peasant, who said:

"Your Highness, many years ago my grandfather told me that in that castle lies a princess, the most beautiful in the world. It was said that she must sleep there for a hundred years, until she is awakened by a kiss from a king's son."

As soon as he heard this, the young prince was determined to see the beautiful princess for himself, and he set off in the direction of the castle.

As he entered the forest, the briars and trees drew back to make a path for him. He found himself in an avenue of great oaks, at the end of which was the castle. Under the trees, deer stood still as statues.

The prince climbed the castle steps and pushed open the door. As he looked into the great hall, he was filled with icy fear. The greenish light that filtered through the leaf-covered windows revealed a strange sight: lords and ladies, some seated, some standing, but all asleep.

Regaining his courage, the prince walked through
room after room of sleeping attendants.

At last he came to a great bedchamber hung with rich tapestries and bathed in the same watery green light. On the bed lay the most beautiful girl he had ever seen. A small dog lay at her feet. Her face was flushed as though she had just fallen asleep after a walk in the garden.

Hardly knowing what he did, the prince leaned forward and kissed her. The princess stirred, opened her eyes, and smiled.

"Is it you, dear prince?" she said.

At that moment, the silence was shattered by the sound of a hundred clocks striking the hour, and the babble of a thousand voices that had not spoken for a hundred years. Puff began to bark shrilly.

Servants jumped to their feet and hurried about their business, the guards took up their arms, and the king and queen rushed to embrace their daughter and the prince.

A wedding was arranged at once, for the two young people had fallen in love at first sight, and there was great rejoicing. The seven good fairies were invited to the marriage feast, but the bad old fairy had died as the princess woke up, and so she could no longer harm anybody.

The prince and princess were married; and by the time they had a little child the princess had no memory at all of her hundred years' sleep, for it seemed like a dream.